Malt Loaf and the Tooth Fairy

Follow the adventures of the cute (and sometimes mischievous) miniature Shetland ponies Sylvie, Molly, Malt Loaf, Milly, Echo, Crunchy, Minstrel, Gypsy, the slightly bigger (and sometimes grumpy) Malcolm, and their gentle Dartmoor pony friend Fred (who loves to pull a pony carriage).

They are the Happy Ponies, and they live on a diamond-shaped island somewhere in the south of England.

www.HappyPonyStories.com

"Good morning everyone!" Molly shouted to the ponies as she trotted across the field towards Malt Loaf.

"Hello Malt Loaf," said Molly as she screeched to a halt beside her best friend. Malt Loaf was trying to nibble a tuft of grass and looked quite sad.

"Malt Loaf, what's the matter? You look very unhappy." Molly was getting quite concerned.

"It's my tooth, it keeps wobbling when I try to eat," replied Malt Loaf.

Molly left Malt Loaf trying to eat the grass and ran over to where Sylvie was lying down. "Great Aunt Sylvie! Great Aunt Sylvie! Malt Loaf isn't feeling well! Oh dear, I don't know what to do!"

Poor Molly was running round and round in circles muttering to herself "What am I to do? What am I to do?"

"Molly!" replied Sylvie sharply, "tell me exactly what the matter is with Malt Loaf and for goodness sake, stand still, you are making me quite dizzy." Sylvie felt her eyes rolling all over the place as she watched Molly.

Molly stopped spinning and began to tell Sylvie about Malt Loaf and how she couldn't eat properly.

Fred and Malcolm, having heard Molly shouting, appeared from behind the big tree to see what was going on. Mrs Squirrel looked down through the branches and Mrs Hedgehog peeked out from under the blackberry hedge to hear more.

"Hello Great Aunt Sylvie. Morning all." Said Fred.

"What's all the fuss about?" Malcolm asked.

"It's Malt Loaf," Sylvie replied. "She is having trouble eating. I just hope that she hasn't cut her mouth on anything."

"You stay here," Fred said. "Malcolm and I will go over to her and see how we can help."

Fred and Malcolm walked over to Malt Loaf who was still trying to eat. As they got nearer, they could see lumps of soggy wet grass on the floor. Malt Loaf looked up as they approached.

"I wish I knew what was wrong with me." Malt Loaf said sadly.

Fred and Malcolm exchanged glances, "I think we know what the problem is," said Fred. "But to be sure, go and speak to Great Aunt Sylvie. She will know what to do."

Malt Loaf agreed and slowly walked over to Sylvie. Sylvie could immediately see how worried Malt Loaf looked.

"There, there," Sylvie said softly, "tell me what the problem is." Sylvie listened while Malt Loaf explained that her tooth felt really wobbly, which was making the grass fall out of her mouth as she couldn't chew it properly.

"Great Aunt Sylvie am I really ill?" Malt Loaf sounded very frightened. Sylvie chuckled quietly to herself. "Oh Malt Loaf, of course you're not ill. I am sure I know what the problem is. Please can you open your mouth so I can have a look?"

Malt Loaf opened her mouth wide. "Yes, I can see now," Sylvie stated. "Hmm, just what I thought." Malt Loaf was getting very panicky. "Oh dear is it bad?"

"You'll be fine" Sylvie reassured her. "When you are young your very first set of teeth are called baby teeth."

"Baby teeth, oh I see," Malt Loaf interrupted.

7

"You are growing and your baby teeth are too small now. They will come out and be replaced by your second teeth, your grown up teeth. When your wobbly tooth falls out you will feel much better and food will stop falling out of your mouth."

Malt Loaf was relieved. "Great Aunt Sylvie what do I do with my tooth when it does fall out? What if I eat it by mistake?" She asked.

"I doubt you will do that," Sylvie replied. "Now, have you heard of the Tooth Fairy?"

"No. Who is the Tooth Fairy?" said Molly, her eyes wide with excitement. "Does she have wings and fly?"

"Yes," continued Sylvie, "the Tooth Fairy has to get to children and ponies all over the world, so she has to be able to get around very quickly."

As the day progressed Malt Loaf was feeling a lot happier even though her tooth was still wobbling away in her mouth.

"Is this tooth ever going to fall out?" she thought impatiently. "I wonder if the Tooth Fairy knows where I live? She must be very clever to know when my tooth falls out."

The sun was about to disappear behind the hills as evening approached. Tara appeared round the corner of the stables. She filled the water bucket and refilled the ponies haynets. Then she walked over to where Fred, Malcolm, Minstrel, Crunchy, Milly, Echo, Sylvie, Gypsy, Molly and Malt Loaf were standing and gave them all a treat.

"Good night ponies," she said. "I can see you are all okay. Have you had a good day?" Malt Loaf looked at Fred and Malcolm and whispered, "If only she knew!"

The ponies gathered together ready to sleep under the big tree, which acted like a big umbrella if it rained. Malt Loaf joined them although she kept thinking that she should really stay in the yard, just in case her tooth fell out so she could put it under her haynet for the Tooth Fairy to find. She still had the treat that Tara had given them in her mouth. It was a soft treat and she had decided she could suck it slowly so it didn't hurt her tooth.

All of a sudden… "IT'S OUT, IT'S OUT - HOORAY!" The ponies all jumped up and stood with their ears pricked forwards watching Malt Loaf jumping up and down, staring at her tooth on the ground in front of her.

"My tooth has come out! I can put it under my haynet and the Tooth Fairy will come and then I will get my apple or carrot. Yippee!" Malt Loaf couldn't contain her excitement. She ran and skipped all around the field.

"Calm down please Malt Loaf," Malcolm grumbled.

Malt Loaf was bubbling with excitement. "I've lost my tooth! I've lost my tooth!"

"Great Aunt Sylvie," Minstrel said, "please have a word with her, she is really being a nuisance."

"Minstrel and all of you, be patient with her, Malt Loaf is only young. After tonight she will be her usual self again," said Sylvie.

"Come on Malt Loaf," said Echo to her daughter. "Let's go and put your tooth under your haynet." Echo carefully picked up Malt Loaf's tooth with her mouth and together they walked to the yard. Echo put the tooth into a little bag which she hid under Malt Loaf's haynet.

"I wonder if I will see the fairy?" thought Malt Loaf as they settled down for the night. She tried and tried to stay awake to see the fairy, but her eyes were really tired and eventually she fell asleep.

Malt Loaf thought she was dreaming. She could hear a fluttering sound and it appeared to be coming from near her haynet. Slowly she half opened her eyes and stood as still and as quietly as she could.

As her eyes adjusted to the darkness she saw a tiny light flickering by the stable where the haynet was hanging. The haynet suddenly moved and the special bag that had her tooth in it was floating in mid-air.

"That light must be the Tooth Fairy!" She thought. Malt Loaf could see twinkling fairy dust sparkling in the moonlight. She watched as the fluttering light drifted out of the yard. Malt Loaf jumped to her feet and ran to the gate and watched as the light faded down the lane and then disappeared.

Malt Loaf returned to her haynet and nuzzled it out of the way, where she saw a carrot and an apple.

"I saw the Tooth Fairy!" She thought. "I actually saw her! I can't wait to tell the others."

When morning arrived Malt Loaf couldn't wait any longer. She bounded across to where the others were.

"Great Aunt Sylvie, all of you, I saw the Tooth Fairy when she came last night!" Malt Loaf described what she had seen. The ponies listened quietly.

"And look!" said Malt Loaf. "I have an apple and a carrot, which I am going to share with all of you!"

"Thank you Malt Loaf, that's very kind," said Malcolm and the other ponies.

"Just one thing," said Great Aunt Sylvie. "Remember it is very important that you look after your teeth. You should brush them twice a day and let the dentist see your teeth regularly."

"What's a dentist?" Asked Molly. Malcolm groaned. "Don't these children know anything?!" he stated.

"You'll see Molly," said Sylvie. "I heard Jim saying that the pony dentist is coming to see us soon."

They all tucked into the apple and carrot. Even Malt Loaf could eat it now as her mouth was feeling a lot better.

"I can't wait until my tooth falls out," said Molly. The ponies all laughed. "Silly Molly," they said.

A couple of days later, Tara and Jim brought all the ponies into the yard. "What's happening?" asked Malt Loaf. There was a strange man in the yard who began talking to Tara and Jim and he was carrying a large bag.

"Do you remember I told you that the pony dentist was coming to see us? Well today is the day for his visit." Replied Sylvie.

"Oh, will I like that?" Malt Loaf's voice trembled. "Yes, you will be fine," said Echo reassuringly. "You will have to open your mouth wide so he can see your teeth. He might give them a little clean and that might tickle a little bit. There really is nothing to be frightened of at all."

Malt Loaf looked nervously at the bag that the dentist had started to unpack. It was full of different instruments, and then, much to her surprise, he put a torch on a band around his head!

23

The pony dentist turned around and spoke to all the ponies. "Hello ponies," he said in a kind voice. "Who is going first?"

Tara suggested that Sylvie went first, as Sylvie is the oldest and had seen the dentist a lot of times. Tara thought that she would set a good example to the young ponies about how to stand still and open your mouth wide.

One by one, the pony dentist looked at the ponies' teeth. Malt Loaf and Molly still felt nervous, but stood very still as the dentist looked into their mouths with his torch and prodded at their teeth with his metal instrument. It didn't hurt at all.

"Well," said the dentist when he had finished looking at the ponies. "I am very impressed, all your teeth are looking very good. I can see that you brush them regularly, well done!."

The dentist gave Malt Loaf and Molly a sticker which had a picture of a bright shiny tooth. The young ponies grinned.

It was time for the dentist to go. "Goodbye ponies, you have all been very good," he said as he drove away. All the ponies whinnied, "Goodbye."

Tara and Jim gave all the ponies some apples as a treat before untying them and letting them back into the field. The ponies galloped away together.

"That was fun. It didn't hurt at all!" shouted Molly to Malt Loaf. "Yes it was – I hope he'll be back soon!" Replied Malt Loaf.

"Hmm, not too soon. He disturbs my afternoon nap!" Said Malcolm.

All the ponies laughed.

The end.